Edward Augustus Horton

DISCOURSE DELIVERED to the FIRST PARISH in HINGHAM

Edward Augustus Horton

DISCOURSE DELIVERED to the FIRST PARISH in HINGHAM

ISBN/EAN: 9783741123757

Manufactured in Europe, USA, Canada, Australia, Japa

Cover: Foto ©Andreas Hilbeck / pixelio.de

Manufactured and distributed by brebook publishing software
(www.brebook.com)

Edward Augustus Horton

DISCOURSE DELIVERED to the FIRST PARISH in HINGHAM

Edward Augustus Horton

DISCOURSE DELIVERED to the FIRST PARISH in HINGHAM

DISCOURSE

DELIVERED TO

THE FIRST PARISH IN HINGHAM

ON THE

Two Hundredth Anniversary

OF THE

OPENING OF ITS MEETING-HOUSE FOR PUBLIC WORSHIP.

SUNDAY, JANUARY 8, 1882.

BY REV. EDWARD AUGUSTUS HORTON.

With an Appendix.

———◆———

HINGHAM:

PUBLISHED BY THE PARISH.

1882.

DISCOURSE

DELIVERED TO

THE FIRST PARISH IN HINGHAM

ON THE

TWO HUNDREDTH ANNIVERSARY OF THE OPENING
OF ITS MEETING-HOUSE FOR PUBLIC WORSHIP.

CONTENTS.

𝔄𝔭𝔭𝔢𝔫𝔡𝔦𝔵.

Committee on Publication.

DISCOURSE.

DISCOURSE.

"GOD BE WITH US AS HE WAS WITH OUR FATHERS." I *Kings*, viii. 57.

NO more expressive prayer could we offer this morning than the one breathed by my text. God *was* with the little colony of heroic spirits who planted this town, and reared this meeting-house. We assemble to remember that Providential guidance, to revive the lustre of a noble history, and thus quicken all deep and noble sentiments. I cannot promise you I shall be brief, for that seems neither just to you nor to the subject. I will not impair the dignity and scope of my theme by headlong brevity. Two centuries we are to traverse, a marvellous record to revive; there is justice to be done, and fit lessons are to be drawn. True, much of the historical material on which I must rely has been printed; but it is not accessible; the young know it not. From such sources I shall draw only those portions which seem necessary to the right proportion of my remarks. We may well linger, and spare not our words, as the two-hundredth anniversary of this ancestral sanctuary passes by. Not for a half century probably will you have another important anniversary; and so many of us will not be here! Where is there an edifice of any kind in this land so thronged with memories, so rich in associations, so suggestive to patriot, worshipper, poet, orator, or preacher? Faneuil Hall speaks of patriotism; the Old South recalls one era of religious struggle; King's Chapel tells the first victory of Episcopacy in New England; some old dwelling-house represents a distinct family; but this structure is calculated, by past uses and scenes, — so varied, so significant, so far-extended, — to kindle every heart and stir the entire range of emotions.

Without further preface let me proceed to the pleasant duty before us. With what a sigh we read that one, short sentence in Hobart's Diary, under date of January 8, 1681:[1] "This Sabbath we first met in the new meeting-house." How much more we crave to know! We know to-day what has been confirmed for some time, — thanks to the diligent investigations of lovers of history! — that the old meeting-house which bore the palisade's protection, and had sufficed for the early life of Hingham, was outgrown; that in deciding upon the best location for a new one, disagreements arose, and the state authorities intervened; that at last the spot where we are assembled was chosen, and the work went forward. We know the names of those who had seats in the new house, and in what order. In a general way we can picture the interior. It was devoid of plastering, without a ceiling; there was but one pew in the whole house, the rest of the space being filled with benches; there was no paint. We know that two children were baptized on that first Sunday, and their

[1] Old style.

names survive. We know that infants were often
baptized the day they were born, and one of these
babes may have received the holy rites on its natal day.
There was a bell that summoned the worshippers. At
first a drum had been beaten, or a shell blown, or a
flag hoisted, to indicate the hour of service, but Hingham had long employed a bell. These are things
within the pale of certainty. But beyond is the twi-
light of conjecture. What was the text of Mr. Norton's
sermon? What psalms were sung? Did any friends
from other towns join the assembly? Was there an
offering of the people's money on that day? How was
the service conducted, and in what features did it differ
from ours to-day?

In response to these questions no distinct answers
come back. Shall we give imagination permission to
paint what history has not recorded? For there can
hardly be a more attractive subject for us this morning
than the picture of the first religious service ever held
in this venerable edifice. Let us fill out the unknown
parts by touches of probability. Mr. Norton is the
young minister; Peter Hobart died three years before
this meeting-house was opened. There is strong proof
that Norton preached his own ordination sermon, still
preserved, which occurred two months before the aged
Hobart died. As this Sunday dawns, two hundred
years ago, the town wakes to an unusual stir and
earnestness. The extremely aged exert their slumber-
ing wills and go to the new meeting-house; the young
gaze with admiration at the structure; a feeling of pride

and a sense of gratitude rule in the mature men who have carried their hopes to completion. The minister comes. He wears a gown, for his scholarly tastes would lead him to do that. The robe among the Puritans was the scholar's garment, whether worn by judge, professor, or preacher. An hour-glass stands on the pulpit; the people are all assembled; a hush comes over the congregation. Mr. Norton rises and offers a prayer. It is the one long prayer in the whole service, delivered slowly, impressively. The pastor remembers the past and renders thanks for deliverance, for present blessings. He prays for many, very many things, for many, very many persons, — for the young, the old, the sick, the bereaved. The sands of the hour-glass run on and mark more than half an hour in time from the beginning of the prayer. It ends ; a man, the guardian of order in the assembly, steps forward and turns the glass, as it is out. It is evident that there are to be no dedicatory services. Our forefathers avoided even the suspicion of popish habits, and would not yield to sentiment in consecrating a building, lest it should seem like the superstition of the Mother Church at Rome. So the service proceeds as on any Sunday, unmarked save by the glow of feeling in every heart, and the universal tokens of newness. The reading of Scriptures follows. When ministers read the Bible in the pulpit, and did not explain as they went along, it was called "dumb reading." The people of Hingham were averse to it, as were most congregations ; so Mr. Norton expounds as he proceeds, and coming upon a passage which refers to God's reward of the faithful, he enlarges upon it, applying the text to the flock before him. A psalm is given out. There are no appointed singers, no instruments, no tune-books. The congregation, indeed, know but six or seven tunes, among them St. Martin's. These, however, they know well; and as the psalm is lined, a resonant voice, near the deacons' seat, takes up the tune which all expect; and the simple, grand notes go sounding up to the rafters, and thaw the chilly air, and set free the heart's pent-up emotion. In standing to sing, the congregation obtains some release from the cold conditions of the fireless room. In the only pew are Mrs. Peter Hobart and Mrs. Norton. The widow, it is noticed, becomes affected. No doubt memory is busy, and she thinks of her lost companion, who would have rejoiced to see this day and the glory of this house. At last the whole psalm has been sung, and the sermon follows. It is in substance. we may believe, an exhortation to remember the faith and be loyal to it. The worshippers are reminded that with a great price this liberty and true doctrine were purchased. They are bidden to shun all ease in Zion, now that this new and sumptuous sanctuary spreads such temptations to pride and satisfaction. The discourse was long, but Matthew Hawke did not preserve it in short hand, and we can only imagine its force and pertinency. Another psalm is sung, and after prayer the impressive benediction sends the large congregation away until the afternoon, — when the two children are baptized, one or two men speak after the sermon, and a collection is taken, the minister saying, " as God hath prospered you, so freely give." Such a picture may be drawn with every reason for believing in its truthfulness.

Touching as the scene is, it receives an added pathos when we remember that our fathers had acquaintance with splendor. The old church at Hingham, England, and all the ancient glory of cathedral and minster in the Old Home were familiar to them. This simple structure had been hewn from the wilderness, not by barbaric hands, ignorant of taste, beauty, grandeur, but by those who, as they entered this house for the first time, realized deeply what they had paid for liberty of conscience and human rights. Yet they abated not one jot or tittle of courage and hope.

It will be seen that the first service, in its essential characteristics, did not differ materially from ours to-day.

Little thought Deacon John Leavitt and Deacon John Smith, as they sat in their prominent seats, centre of all eyes, that we, down the long vista of two centuries, would also look at them. The same names are represented in the pews this morning that were known then, — descendants in unbroken lines, one family having worshipped here consecutively for ten generations. It seems as though but a few years had elapsed, and we were celebrating a recent event. The remote epochs rush together, true kinship of spirit asserts itself; and, instead of commemorating a dim, decayed and lustreless transaction, we seem to participate in the

first religious service of this sanctuary. This, however, is the uplifted mood of thought and sympathy,
that transcendent power by which we ally ourselves
with all that is noble and lovable in the past. Slowly
we descend and touch again the facts, the outward
realities of life. We *are* commemorating something
which occurred so long ago that the mind grows be-
wildered as it endeavors to trace the vicissitudes of
the intervening decades. It will be profitable for us
to recall some historic conditions which existed when
these walls first rose. They are very interesting; but
they lead on to that more valuable story of what
transpired in religious affairs after the meeting-house
was opened.

Soon after the erection of this meeting-house,
progressive measures multiplied in New England, and
ministers assumed new functions. Before 1686, ministers had been prohibited from performing the marriage
ceremony. In that year, four years after the completion
of this edifice, the Governor issued a proclamation
authorizing ministers to share what before only the
civil magistrates had liberty to do. Three years after
this house was built, we find that a minister offered
prayer at a funeral, — the first instance on record. The
burial of the beloved dead had been a cold and sad
transaction. Only the friends gathered at an appointed
time in the home, and without prayer, without singing,
without service of any kind, the body was borne to the
grave and buried. The reasons for this custom were
founded on a desire to show aversion to superstition.

It was held that prayer at a funeral might have an appearance of Popery, inasmuch as in the Romish Church prayers were said for the dead and over the dead. And the denial to the clergy of the right of solemnizing marriages arose from the same source, — that it might savor of a sacrament. These things were changing, and by the year 1700 sermons and prayers grew common at funerals.

So, too, the temper and usage of the people were changing, two hundred years ago, from the early rigor. Preachers found fault with the evidences of taste and comfort already springing up in the more prosperous families. I doubt not the criticism was over-severe. Urian Oakes in his Election Sermon of 1673, — nine years before the opening of this meeting-house, — put forth this remark, which shows that the old-time preachers were often as sensational as the modern. He said: "When persons spend more time in trimming their bodies than their souls, then you may say of them, as a worthy divine wittily speaks, that they are like the cinnamon tree — nothing good but the bark."

This trait grew so prominent in the custom of giving gloves and rings and scarfs at funerals, that a law was passed, about forty years after the completion of this building, restricting excesses. A wise act, for we learn that at the funeral of Governor Belcher's wife over a thousand pairs of gloves were bestowed on relatives and friends. The ministers always had large stores of rings, gifts from bereaved parishioners. Humanity is the same in all times. It has its excess under one form or another. While we marvel at the extravagance which led to such an abuse as this of old, we ourselves develop the same trait in the over-use of flowers at funerals, evoking requests on all hands to withhold them.

It is often alleged that the Puritan was exceptionally rigid in his views of church-going, and that our New England laws were unusually severe. This is not so. The Cavalier in Virginia was more compulsory. In 1610 a law was passed that every colonist in Virginia should attend church twice every Sunday. Failing in this, for the first offence he must lose allowance for a week; for the second offence, lose allowance and be whipped; for the third offence he should suffer death! It is often supposed, too, that the Puritan was extremely Mosaic and terrible in his legal penalties for crime. In reality he was merciful compared to Old England, where, in the eighteenth century, as many as two hundred and twenty-three offences were punishable with death. The Puritan simply said to many offenders: "Depart! go elsewhere! take your life and try to make it better in some new place."

Let us grant that the Puritans were strict. Had they not just cause? The men of every era are to be judged by *their* environment, not by ours. What was the Puritans' situation?

They had everything at stake. To endanger the dear-bought privileges was beyond question a step no earnest man could permit. Children may be fickle

2

and inconstant of purpose, but not such iron wills as those that cleft the rock of old-time opposition and persecution. They were troubled, too, by bad characters. Ever hovering about their village were such as had come from England hoping to live on the prosperity of the toilers and faithful.

Again, our forefathers were logical. No fancy brought them here, no idle dream. Great hopes shone on their pathway, but they knew how each step must be taken. They have been criticised for demanding liberty of conscience for themselves, yet often denying it to others. Does not the same ground of accusation exist to-day? Can you support this church, and carry out the principle of liberty of conscience to any and every extent? Would you not be at war within yourself as an organization by permitting those to have power and sway in the administration of this parish who might deny, or ridicule, or ignore some of your fundamental beliefs? You say to-day, as they said of old: "Go thy way! Plant for yourself, build for yourself, — but do not enter in to reap where you have not sowed, or tear down what others have arduously built." The truth is that very much of the opprobrium cast on the Puritan for his supposed persecution of others arose more from civil complications than from religious quarrels. Roger Williams's notable case sprang more from his meddling with politics than from his divergence in the way of doctrine. Even in such instances, which would have been called treason in older countries, the Puritan magistrate simply banished, simply cast out elements which he considered dangerous to the welfare of Church and State.

Not to be forgotten is the final argument in the Puritan's behalf. He was a Calvinist. He was a part of that mighty movement which swept over Western Europe and rallied every man who "hated a lie." Calvinism was one of the most significant phases of the new life which has marked modern times. Tersely says Froude the historian: "Whatever exists at this moment in England and Scotland of conscientious fear of doing evil is the remnant of the convictions which were branded by the Calvinists into the people's hearts." Never will this spirit appear again in the harsh dreadful dogmas that appalled and enslaved the mind at times ; but wherever bold reformers strike, wherever the voice of a Carlyle is heard, wherever men say with Matthew Arnold that conduct is three fourths of life, wherever man is rallied to a high, overpowering sense of duty by an incarnated conscience, — there the spirit still exists that animated the Puritans.

Neither was the Puritan so cheerless and smileless as superficial scrutiny reports. Even the pulpit ventured to be witty. Homes were scenes of merry-making ; youth had its games and recreative hours. Deacons played ball together, no longer than sixty years ago, on set days. The old thanksgivings were full of innocent frolic. The "morose, tyrannical, sour visage" tradition assigns to the typical Puritan is misleading. There were some of that cast, as there are now. It is a falla-cious course which leads one to interpret domestic life,

social customs, and personal traits of any period by its
printed creeds, or excessive sermons, or reactionary
utterances. There was not enough sunshine in the
Puritan's life, but there was a great deal; and it steadily
deepened as his lot was ameliorated.

The fitness of Congregationalism for the creation
of this Republic was never more powerfully proven
than by that orator, Hon. Robert C. Winthrop, — our
pride at Yorktown, himself a Churchman, — in his
oration at Plymouth in 1870. It was the only system
by which such a community as New England could
have been organized. "From its fundamental thought
that all Christian men are 'kings and priests unto God,'
sprang popular government in Church and State." We
are celebrating to-day not the death of the Puritan's
idea and his system, but its fulfilment. Its principles
are at the basis of every Protestant denomination in
our land; even the American Episcopal Church has
engrafted some of its features on its polity. It is safe
to say, viewing everything, — the people, their spirit,
their system, — that God was with them peculiarly,
making future results sure.

I am not attempting to transform the defects of the
Puritans into virtues. They were far from perfect.
But they seem to me providential men, set to do a
work — none more difficult in all the world's history.
Had they been characters less vigorous, less tenacious,
less firm and severe, I know not what the history of
this country might have been. It was this tremendous
will that gave us Sam Adams, to face the foreign foe.

It was this stern fidelity that gave us the Mathers, who from their pulpits made the people resolute and God-fearing. It ran like flame in the town-meetings when fresh oppression came, and its avalanche-sweep bore down on the English troops at many a contested field. It is not for us to criticise the Puritan, but to look at him and ask the question: Are we as faithful to the needs of our times?

The Pilgrims and the Puritans came from enlightened, progressive sources. Out of twenty-seven ministers settled at the same time in Massachusetts Bay Colony, Peter Hobart among them, fourteen had graduated from Cambridge, England, four had studied at Oxford, and the others were marked by capable minds. The laity were equally elevated in character, for it might be predicated, did we not know the names of many of them, that no body of men and women, ignorant and narrow, could support such a clergy, give them life, and live on their utterances. It must be remembered that our forefathers did not get away from discussion and peculiar views by coming to this continent. All the questions that agitate us either sprung up among them, or were brought over by new visitors. In 1648 two Indians went to Providence and returned. As they were students under Eliot, the missionary, they reported to him the ideas they had heard. "How is it," they asked, "that with the same Bible, these people in Providence hold such different views from ourselves? They say there is no hell or heaven except in bad or good people's hearts, that baptism of children

is useless, that ministers and magistrates are need-
less." Such extreme views were familiar enough. We
must remember that a people with busy brains are
always developing the same great issues in every age,
under one form and another. Hingham had already
commenced a revolt, in Hobart's day, and certain
Church of England adherents were appealing to
Parliament for their rights to Episcopal services.

Andros, the tyrannical, was after all the unconscious
instrument of a great idea; and while he troubled the
Puritans, he effected freedom for King's Chapel, and
widened liberty of worship. It was in 1700 that the
Brattle Street Church of Boston was formed, after war-
fare and bitterness because the new church would not
promise to conform to every former doctrine and custom. Why, when this building rose, the land was ripe
for stirring changes. Fifty years had imparted an
impetus to the Puritan ideas, and they were fulfilling
their logical destiny.

It is interesting to note how large a part the religious
element assumed in the days we have been considering.
In 1694 two sums were voted by this town for every
public need: $425 were appropriated for the support
of the ministry, and only $225 for all other expenses
in the town! Twenty years before this a law of the
Commonwealth was in force that required every town
to provide a dwelling-house for the minister. If the
minister was not duly and adequately paid, each
county court was required to take measures to have
the deficiencies supplied.

How completely from the beginning this meeting-house was the centre of civil and religious transactions in this town, is seen by a brief glance at the facts. The very Sunday on which the first service occurred, and these beams were echoing God's praise, the hearts of the men were burdened with anxiety. The mother country was threatening to take away the charter of the colony, because of alleged misdemeanors, and with that charter went all titles and claims to the land on which homes and sanctuaries rested. These they had toiled for, and set like jewels in the wilderness. All New England was profoundly stirred. At last, when the threat was executed and the rights of the people swept away, a fast was proclaimed. Every meeting-house was filled with a sad, tearful, prayerful congregation. Of all those houses this is the only one now in existence, its walls made sacred by that bitter, indignant hour. Then followed town-meetings, held here, as they were for one hundred years. The people rallied. Those who rarely spoke here rose and offered the pungent advice, the sturdy sense, of their loyal hearts. Here were considered the grave questions of resistance, self-government, justice, liberty. Yes! the first uses of this building were for such deliberations as arise only when a people's precious privileges are in danger from tyranny, and the sky of the future is black with perils. This old meeting-house was baptized as the home of civil and ecclesiastical liberty by the scenes which earliest transpired in it. On Sundays, beyond doubt, the preacher took his topic many times from the exciting, overshadowing themes of the week. He exhorted, he reasoned, he prayed, all for the endangered cause. And on that signal day in May, after years of anxiety and trial, when the men of Hingham gathered here and elected Daniel Cushing and Thomas Andrews to represent them in the Council of Safety, no doubt Norton was present, and invoked divine blessings on the bold act. It was a daring deed, — as direct a defiance of England as the Revolutionary measures. They risked all, those men of Hingham, then representing nearly two hundred families. Some had been in King Philip's War; some were old, ready to leave the world, but not ready to go without a manly protest against wrong. All these veterans held not back from fresh dangers. It was so throughout the colony. Of all the buildings existing at that time in which this heroic stand was taken, — which saved our land as much as the Revolution, — the patriot finds only this one remaining, upon which he may cast his admiring look, and honor as he treads in reverential mood the spot consecrated by undaunted religious faith.

Any expanded reference to the ministers who have served this parish is uncalled for, so familiar are their characters to you, — their long pastorates, their uniform excellence, their crowns of reward. Yet a quick review of some facts not generally known is fitting. Peter Hobart, who never entered this building, cannot be dissociated from it. He labored, and others entered into his labors. We all know the allusion on

record to his boldness in speaking his mind. Cotton
Mather says one or two other things about him which
bring his character out more distinctly. He always
studied standing, thinking that habit a more diligent
and lively manner of improving time. If I mistake not,
Calvin Lincoln had the same habit in a degree. We
are also told that Mr. Hobart always heard the sermons
of other ministers graciously, as though he truly
worshipped God thereby, — a virtue in a preacher of
highest rank, and in this case proving the truth of the
oft-heard proverb, that the boldest speakers are frequently the most docile listeners.

We must remember in our honor to Hobart that he
gave several sons to the ministry, "worthy preachers,"
we are informed, in Cotton Mather's day. With Hobart was associated Robert Peck, teacher, for three
years, from 1638 to 1641. This cultured man returned
to England, and there resumed preaching.[1]

Of John Norton we have already spoken, — a faithful pastor, a gentle spirit, loving the mild, persuasive
paths of his profession. We are not surprised to find
that he stands forth the only poet in the list of ministers. His sermons are lost; less can be recalled of his
pulpit utterances than of those of any other; but his
poem on Anne Bradstreet gives him a place in the
annals of American literature, and by that he lives in a
national fame. Mr. Norton's pastorate covers that
important period in our Colonial history when a new
people, so to say, came upon the stage. Up to the time

[1] See Appendix.

this meeting-house was reared, the active men and
women had been those born in England, — Americans, but emigrants.   After 1682, we see the native-
born Americans assuming control, — children of the
New World, products of the environment, trained in
the genius of the New World.   They called England
home, but had never seen it.

Therefore, when Ebenezer Gay became minister, we
find a more distinctively original work going on.   We
are not surprised to learn that he was the first Unitarian minister of New England.   The criticism of him
was not concerning what he preached, but what he
omitted to preach.   When Whitefield traversed the
country with such remarkable commotions, Dr. Gay
refused to invite him to Hingham.   The parish wished
to hear him, and appointed one man to see their pastor
and persuade him to send an invitation.   The result
was that the subject was not even broached; and the
loyal man preferred to bear obloquy from his fellow
parishioners, rather than elicit a distinct refusal from
Dr. Gay, and so create a ferment in the parish.   We all
know Gay's ability; over a score of his sermons were
printed, the " Old Man's Calendar," outranking them
all.   The oddity of the pulpit exists in all ages under
some form, and is not peculiar to our age.   Think of
a text like this, used for a sermon by Dr. Gay, delivered
before the Ancient and Honorable Artillery Company:
" I saw by night, and behold, a man riding upon a red
horse, and he stood among the myrtle trees that were
in the bottom ; and behind him were there red horses,

speckled and white." (Zech. i. 8.) Beyond doubt, Dr.
Gay's strong mental power did much to mould the
youth, elevate scholarly traits and perpetuate learning
in a new civilization beset with material cares. The
endowment of a professorship at Harvard College
by Dr. Hersey, and the subsequent foundation by
Madam Derby of an Academy in this town, may justi-
fiably be traced to Dr. Gay's influence.

Henry Ware came to this pulpit as the echoes of the
Revolution were dying away; when Hingham was
rebuilding her fortunes, mourning for her dead, celebrating her heroes, and, above all, glorying in the fame
of her son, Benjamin Lincoln, the friend of Washing-
ton, and one of the deacons of this church. In this
house he was christened, and here his character was
greatly moulded. Dr. Ware was pure, noble, devoted,
spiritual. He was very diffident, —always trembling as
he commenced Sunday service. One habit of his stands
out in striking contrast to the ministerial procrastina-
tion of to-day. He never went to sleep Sunday night
until he had secured his text and subject for the following Sunday.

In 1755, during his predecessor's pastorate, the interior of this audience-room was greatly changed by the
removal of the oaken benches, except in the centre of
the floor, the substitution of high, square pews, together
with some other alterations. Now, under Ware, a pro-
posal was made to build a new meeting-house. This,
fortunately, was not carried out, but important changes
were made in the exterior appearance. In the midst

of these changes, typical of the enlarged and more restless condition of the community, Dr. Ware accepted a professorship at Harvard, and resigned. To him succeeded Joseph Richardson. His pastorate began with the opening century, and terminated but a little over ten years ago. He was once elected to Congress. He was a man of strong feelings, which he ruled with a moral mastery. His knowledge of human nature was large; his ability to deal with practical themes, exceptional. His power to console the sorrowing, and to recall the dead in tender expressions, was also marked. The path he trod was stormy in its inception, and it ended in a storm of physical infirmity; but candor, while it deals no more with the outgrown disputes of the past, will accredit Richardson with heroism, fidelity, self-control, and loyal service to this ancient parish.

After Richardson, the man of fiery action, came Lincoln, the saint, long before the junior pastor and the chief worker. His loss is fresh in our memories, and his absence to-day casts its shadow on our exercises. Yet why should it? Was not his death fitting in circumstance, and beautiful? I seem to feel his presence here; I seem to have the support of his invisible participation. Under Calvin Lincoln another great change took place in this house, and the square pews were removed. To those who do not go back to the beginning of things, this alteration seems very innovating; but let us remember that these present pews are nearer the original benches and seats of this meeting-house

than the box pews. You have returned somewhat to
the church of 1682. Calvin Lincoln needs no eulogy
or description from me at this time and in this pulpit.
He was a part of your homes, the life of this place.
The young loved his benignant face, the aged cherished
his kindly hand, the troubled were soothed by his
gentle accents, and all men turned respectfully to the
light of his character. Calvin Lincoln had from nature
the gift of serene and spiritual traits. The honor to
him is that he was generous in their employment, —
never thinking selfishly of his own happiness, but from
first to last a servant of God's truth and love!

Were there time, the roll of the laity should be
called. The old Congregational democracy which
ushered in this society has ever prevailed. Preacher
and layman act on each other. Conspicuous, also,
has been the career of woman in the past history of
this meeting-house. No one has more feelingly or
justly referred to this fact than he so recently taken
from you, the Hon. Solomon Lincoln, when, in 1835,
he eloquently paid tribute to the mothers of New
England. Vividly he says: "When calamity hung
over the hopes of your fathers in a heavy cloud,
when desolating war carried dismay to the stoutest
hearts, and the smoke of your villages almost darkened
the horizon, when the war-cry of the savage brought
terror to every fireside and crushed the hopes of affec-
tion almost to despair, it was then that the boldest
spirits were sustained, encouraged by the animating
tones of woman's voice and the tender solicitudes of

woman's heart." "Patriotism," he truly adds, "has no exclusive character." Even so, I echo, religion has no exclusive character. It finds its natural allies in woman's sentiments and devotion. It is she who keeps vigils that the Zion of her Church may prosper. It is she who responds to the Sunday bell and teaches its call to her children as heaven's invitation. It is she who preserves where innovation destroys, and who prays where others despair.

This meeting-house has been a home. All that you mean by that word, a word of rich and unmeasured import, has been embodied in the career of this house, by loyal men and women. Think of the scenes it has witnessed! The long procession of the two centuries passes through it. The babe is christened; the same infant, grown old and at rest, is here borne out amid tears. The merry marriage has here shed its joy, — the public man received from this place his recognition, by a mourning community, of "well done, good and faithful servant." Here have been the sincere hand-shakings of thousands of Sundays, here the exposition of nearly every part of Scripture. At times the Holy Ghost has seemed to descend and sway the large congregation. John Cotton, as he preaches in 1684 for Mr. Norton, looks into the eyes of as faithful a band of colonists as can be found in history; and he who speaks to-day beholds worthy descendants of those loyal spirits. We are wont to point to the long duration of pastorates in this parish; there are some prolonged terms of service on the part of the laymen.

Thomas Andrews was treasurer for forty-three years; Ebed Ripley was treasurer thirty-five years; James S. Lewis was clerk for twenty-five years; and your present efficient clerk has already served twenty years. Within the last fifty years you recall Deacon Hobart, Deacon Ripley, — pillars in the church, untiring servitors. I would it were in my power to summon forth some of the men and women on whose shoulders the Ark rested in the days past. To them the ministers turned for advice and encouragement; for their presence in church each Lord's day, the preacher eagerly looked; at their firesides the pastor told his story, and patted the children kindly on the head. Yes! there must have been ever a noble laity in this town, — thoughtful, patient, God-fearing, and earnest. So may the story always be !

I give place here to a list of the deacons of the First Church in Hingham since the opening of this house. Men occupying such positions had, in old times, large influence and reputation. In many instances they were, next to the minister, ruling powers and guides in church affairs.

> John Leavitt, the ancestor of all of that name in this town; John Smith, also known as Captain, an efficient officer in King Philip's War; David Hobart, son of Rev. Peter Hobart, and father of Rev. Nehemiah Hobart, first minister of Cohasset; Benjamin Lincoln, for a long time town clerk; Joshua Hearsey; Solomon Cushing; Joshua Hearsey; Josiah Lincoln; Thomas Andrews; Joseph Thaxter; Benjamin Lincoln, Major-

General in the Revolutionary Army; Benjamin Cushing; William Cushing; Thomas Fearing; Caleb Hobart, who served in the Revolution; Nehemiah Ripley; Caleb Hobart, son of the previous deacon of the same name. Fearing Burr, Henry Siders, and Henry C. Harding, are those now appointed to carry the emblems.

It is an inspiring thought to me that I am not celebrating the end of greatness, but its sustained and ever-widening orbit. In these later years we may proudly parallel the events of the early days. This auditorium witnessed, a few years ago, a scene as impressive as any that ever occurred within its walls. The space was packed with human beings, all moved by one impulse, to render tribute to a good man. When Albert Fearing was buried from this place, the representative elements of this town and the Commonwealth assembled, not to honor mere fame, adventitious wealth, or glory, but to express love and reverence for a philanthropist, — one whose benefactions to this society are embodied in ampler privileges and security. He was one of you, and honors your record. When John A. Andrew's grave was to be adorned by that triumph of sculpture which Gould wrought, into this house the ardent, thrilled audience thronged. Memorable the day also, and the scene, when the "Ancient and Honorable Artillery Company" gathered in this church to pay tribute, not alone to historic memories as venerable as its own, but to recall worthy leaders who once worshipped here. And here the last, affectionate words were spoken to a sympathetic assembly, over the

mortality of him who was Hingham's leading citizen
for so many years, — Solomon Lincoln, who at the age
of twenty-three wrote the history of Hingham, and the
previous year gave the oration on Independence Day.
The good name of your town was dear to him, and he
maintained its reputation in many striking ways. We
cannot forget, among the undying scenes enacted here,
one which the future historian will dwell upon, — that
day, that hour, when your beloved pastor received the
angel of a new life and heard his message here, in
the midst of supplications for our country and its
honored President. How the hands of loving parishioners carried him forth to his home, and the day of
his burial drew a throng of sincere mourners, — all this
is so recent and vivid as to cause emotion.

No tongue or pen will ever tell the tale of those
myriad impressive personal experiences which, from
the Sabbath two hundred years ago, have continued;
but immortal memories have borne them on into
eternity. Who shall dare measure the extent of evil
checked and goodness advanced by the offices of this
sanctuary, — of burdens lightened, tears stanched,
hope quickened, misery alleviated, doubt removed,
heroism inspired, truth instilled? God knows! And
to Him at this hour we reverently give thanks for the
marvellous private, personal soul-history this event
commemorates!

When this meeting-house was located it stood in
the midst of the population. There was also as much
wealth one side as the other. But time changed this;

new precincts were formed, and gradually new meeting-
houses arose.   Do not imagine that a dead uniformity
characterized this part of the South Shore.   In Scituate,
Parson Chauncy, afterward President of Harvard College, practised immersion and divided the parish ; but
when he accepted the presidency he promised to abstain
from disseminating his peculiar views.   Whether he
grew tired of his first opinions, or the new office con-
verted him, I know not.   Hingham sent a peacemaker
to Scituate, who reconciled the factions, and he —
Nicholas Baker — became their minister.   The history
of the successive societies you know.   It is enough to
say that the mother church had no ill-feeling except
in one well-known case.   If there was a reluctance to
let the children go, at any time, it arose from some
complication of taxes, or from an unwillingness to see
the old parish weakened.   But Providence has favored
you, and while contributing to the inauguration of new
parishes, bone of your bone, and blood of your blood,
your own strength has been unimpaired.

Under some circumstances it might be profitable to
you and obligatory on me to trace the doctrinal history
of this church.   But there are certain reasons why
such a recital, except in a very general way, has no
special fitness in a rapid review of the history of the
Old Meeting-house.   This pulpit and this people have
never waged any theological battles.   This church
never had a creed.   Its first covenant was a simple
avowal of Christian fellowship and Christian discipleship.   In this respect it followed a course similar to

many of the early churches. The test of membership
in the church was chiefly one of character. I have
already stated that Dr. Gay was the first minister in
New England in whose preaching we find evidence of
a change from Calvinistic tenets. It is very striking
that King's Chapel, under Rev. James Freeman, was
the first church to array itself openly on the side of
Unitarianism. King's Chapel was the creation of
Andros and his fellow worshippers, who instituted the
first organized Episcopal or Church of England services in New England. King's Chapel was the Tory
Church for a long time; but in 1787 it became openly
Unitarian. Still, to Hingham and to this meeting-
house and to Dr. Gay, over fifty years before, belongs
the credit or discredit, as may be viewed, of initiating
the sentiments and principles which lie at the head-
sources of the Unitarian movement in New England.
I have not the slightest desire to rake over old fires,
or fan flames almost extinct. I speak as a historian.
I can believe that Dr. Gay was often silent on the five
points of Calvin, rather than denunciatory. He probably emphasized the more persuasive and benignant
aspects of religion, — appealed rather than threatened,
reasoned rather than dogmatized, pointed out the
good in everything rather than criticised theology.
I should judge that he might have set the example for
Dr. Freeman by hating bigotry of all kinds, Unitarian
or Orthodox. Dr. Mayhew and Dr. Chauncy of Boston appear after Gay, and just before Freeman, lights
in the new firmament. You might infer that modifica-

tions in views like these betokened a wider change
than individual opinions.   Yes! it was true that the
opening of this meeting-house was coincident with
great fermentation in church doctrines and confessions.
Ministers were modifying their interpretation of the
Lord's Supper and of Baptism.   Arminianism was
springing up.   Whitefield and Jonathan Edwards
gave the churches "great awakenings."   As the years
rolled on, the Universalists appeared in Murray and
Ballou, adding another agitating element to the stirring
drama.   Different kinds of Calvinists appeared, includ-
ing the Hopkinsians.   This type finally became the
well-known New England Theology, while the sterner
form was perpetuated in Presbyterianism.   It does not
appear that the ministers of this church took aggressive
prominence in this intense development of theological
belief, — intense, because heated by personal embitter-
ment, and inflamed by factions that rent our New
England churches in twain.   When the present century
began, strifes deepened; in twenty years the crisis
came.   Channing is there, and Worcester and Ballou
and Stuart and Woods.   Pamphlets reply to pamphlets.   The whole land is roused.   Princeton and
Andover answer Boston and Cambridge.   The echoes
of controversy sound in every home and village.
Parishes quarrel, divide, go to courts.   Ministers fall
out with their parishes, and parishes with their ministers.
Steadily the Unitarian ideas spread, and find adherents;
and with equal steadiness the Trinitarian Congrega-
tionalists draw to their own centres.   This church, so

far as I can trace its history, has never swerved from a
broad, inclusive church covenant of the simplest kind.
It became Unitarian under Dr. Gay, consciously or
unconsciously, and has been of that faith since. While
never concealing its own beliefs, or failing to spread
its banners on the outer walls of denominational work,
it has respected the sacred sincerity and rights of
differing Christians. This pulpit has never wandered
into vagaries, or meddled with idle speculations. It
has never sought destruction and criticism as its glory.
It has assailed no denomination or people, but with
positive and firm utterance proclaimed God a Heav-
enly Father, Christ man's Guide and Savior, the Holy
Spirit our ever-present solace and inspiration. This
meeting-house has, for two hundred years, echoed those
sentiments which exalt man's hopes and reverently
present our Maker, by portraying humanity's inborn
greatness, the beauty of character, the moral atonement,
the eternal hope of the future, and the claims of an
honest, upright, Christian life to an immortal inheritance. Yes! I may cover the entire two centuries, for
I find nothing in Norton to refute my statement. Here
the preachers have taught the nobility of reason, and
the duty of diligence in studying Scripture. Here the
comfort of God's love and his nearness have been
impressed upon the mourner. Youth has heard here
thrilling words of admonition, based on the belief that
God gives to each a mission, and that perfection is
man's goal. Have you departed from the faith con-
signed to us by serious forefathers? No! Outwardly,

it might seem so. Truly, no! We must judge the
Puritan and his meeting-house by the fruits. You are
the Puritans' children, and have tried to be faithful
to the principles they represented. You have been!
Could Hobart arise and be a living part of this last
quarter of the nineteenth century, where do you think
his fellowship would be? With you! Principles grow;
they are not made. You have unfolded the original
truths. I am not strenuous for names, and care not
what we call the victories of religion in the next century; but of this you may be sure, — the face of this
church fronts the light, it walks the sure path. What
is that path? Primarily, it is the logical carrying out
of the principles our forefathers winnowed from old
errors, and brought hither to plant in the soil of a new
Republic. This meeting-house stands for a progressive
Christianity. The Puritan Commonwealth has failed;
it could not be built; but in its place has arisen a
Republic, — glory of the ages, hope of the future.
We to-day are celebrating the religious significance of
this meeting-house. It becomes us to ask, in conclu-
sion, what lessons specially come home? What
constitutes the Puritan's religion of to-day? It seems
no boast to say, as we do in our festal hours, that the
Republic has proved itself capable and enduring. Our
orators justly point to battle-fields, to wise conduct in
public crises, to the reserved power that never seems
to fail our nation. And recently, as eloquence painted
the lessons of Yorktown, amid them all we heard the
pleasing statements of a self-sustaining, growing, and

self-respecting people, which people the United States
certainly are. With this new continent in government
is the new continent of religious belief and life:
freedom in both, equality in both, co-operation in
both, — in both the same perils and the same hopes.
The parallel is close. Men asked: Will the American
people create wise laws? It was also asked: Will they
support worship and religious usages? Will they be
an obedient race, loving order and peace? Will they
reverence sacred things? Will they have a high sense
of citizenship? Will they bring home to themselves
moral laws? Will these builders of new homes respect
the past and link their lives with old-time examples?
On the other hand, will they think seriously of the
future and live not for themselves alone, but for
generations to come? Will they think, will they act,
soberly as well as zealously? Will they write their
history in meteoric lines, or carve it faithfully on time's
granite?

Slowly the questions are being answered in our civil
affairs. The respect of the Old World is at last won.
Our self-regulating power has been tested in so many
ways that the skeptical are softening, and the doubtful
grow assured. Our charters and our constitutions
tell us in simple but impressive language the objects
and principles for which all this national and state
government exists. Let us look a moment at the aims
and laws of religion in a Republic.

The object of a Republic, expressed succinctly, is to
assist each man to the possession and employment of

his best self. The enjoyment of freedom and the pursuit of happiness are means to an end.

This end of realizing the most in each, and of guaranteeing rights to all, is sought by spreading privileges, by opening all paths, by diffusing intelligence and thrift. Naturally the object of the Christian religion, in the midst of such strong incentives would be similar. The ministry of religion in a Republic is to help every one to the knowledge and use of his best self. It is not simply to save him from a future of condemnation, or to conciliate a higher power, or to solace life's wounds, or to settle doubts of mind. These may have been the aims of the past. The supreme goal of a pure Christianity is to make every human being rich, ripe, and full for the duties and the service of a life in this continent. It seeks to open his eyes to everything noble; to strip away bondage of superstition; to spur him with emulation; to unfold every faculty; to put him at work in mankind's service; to tune the single life to the keynote of the highest welfare of all ; to locate in his breast guiding precepts; to turn him from traditions to truths, from fear to love; to create a mighty, overpowering sense of joy in the obeying of God's laws now; to unveil the richness of this universe, and show him how grand a thing it is to explore it; to fill worship with reality and life; to lift him away from morbid retrospect, or vain anticipation, with an eagle's renewed flight, — indeed, to make the one man a loyal citizen of the Divine Republic, which is righteousness, truth, and love.

Out of such religious and civil ideas, which our fathers planted, which they embodied in the uses of this meeting-house, have sprung some ruling sentiments, strong alike in law and theology.

The sacredness of the individual has been enhanced. The spiritual worth of every human being has been increased by humanitarian labor. Man's kinship with a divine source becomes clearer. We are all kings. Man's place in the world is rightly settled. The world was not made solely for man. The old idea of a monarchy favored a crude, crass conception of the universe. What history has to say concerning the human race is now better understood in the light of our institutions.

The object of a Republic is to make citizens, —citizens loyal, true, honest. The object of a Republic's religion is to make character. The old-world view is that religion must be made and presented to the masses. If they refuse it in this dogmatic form, denounce them; if they accept blindly, crown them. For our people we present a boundless hope.

Often will it be necessary for the leaders of the people to recall our attention to the first principles of our national and religious life. Webster's words at Plymouth are ever timely: "Whatever makes men good Christians makes them good citizens. Our fathers came here to enjoy their religion free and unmolested; and at the end of two centuries there is nothing upon which we can express a deeper and more earnest conviction, than of the inestimable importance of that religion to man, both in regard to this life and that which is to come." The progress of our country will not be promoted by discarding religion, but by purifying it of errors, applying its ideas, and incarnating its spirit in systems that shall justify our voluntary elective methods. Come then, with wider reign, a religion of reason and love! Enter, through the portals of the future, a lineage of free worshippers, reverent, ardent, thoughtful! Long may this meeting-house stand, the home of religious liberty and progress; long may its altar flame be fed by loyal hands! Religion shall enfranchise with hope the weak and poor and maimed. It shall be hostile to nothing but crime and wrong and error. From the east and the west, from the north and the south, shall men come and dwell in this Kingdom. "A new heaven and a new earth" shall appear, spread by the hand of Him who maketh all things new.

Turn, great wheels of industry; rise, murmur of cities; ripen, ye harvests of unbounded prairies; circle, with your rumbling wheels, tireless traffic and invention; spread in clustered beauty, spire and dome and turret; but, O beloved land, exhibit also rare deeds of generosity; increase thy list of heroes; kindle new altar flames; enthrone more securely the ideas of truth, love, and justice; and from thy lips never cease to say: "GOD BE WITH US AS HE WAS WITH OUR FATHERS."

Note. — I deem it my duty as well as my pleasure to acknowledge publicly the help I have received from three gentlemen, — zealous and accurate in historical research, — in obtaining material and verifying facts: Mr. Quincy Bicknell, Mr. Fearing Burr, and Mr. George Lincoln. My authorities for statements I cannot give in detail here; they cover many references. The history of the colonial periods is deeply interesting, especially to the people of Hingham.

EDWARD A. HORTON.

APPENDIX.

APPENDIX.

———•———

ORDER OF SERVICES.

January 8, 1882.

———

I. ORGAN VOLUNTARY. (*Batiste.*)

———

II. PASSAGES OF SCRIPTURE.

———

III. HYMN. (*Flint.*)
Sung to the tune of "*Uxbridge.*"

In pleasant lands have fallen the lines
   That bound our goodly heritage ;
And safe beneath our sheltering vines
   Our youth is blessed, and soothed our age.

What thanks, O God, to thee are due,
   That thou didst plant our fathers here ;
And watch and guard them as they grew,
   A vineyard to the planter dear.

The toils they bore, our ease have wrought ;
   They sowed in tears, in joy we reap ;
The birthright they so dearly bought
   We 'll guard till we with them shall sleep.

Thy kindness to our fathers shown,
   In weal and woe, through all the past,
Their grateful sons, O God ! shall own,
   While here their name and race shall last.

IV. SCRIPTURE READING.

AND Solomon stood before the altar of the Lord, in the presence of all the congregation of Israel, and spread forth his hands toward heaven :

And he said : Lord God of Israel, there is no God like thee, in heaven above, or on earth beneath, who keepest covenant and mercy with thy servants that walk before thee with all their heart.

If thy people go out to battle against their enemy, whither-soever thou shalt send them, and shall pray unto the Lord toward the city which thou hast chosen, and toward the house that I have built for thy name,

Then hear thou in heaven their prayer and their supplication, and maintain their cause.

If they sin against thee (for there is no man that sinneth not), and thou be angry with them and deliver them to the enemy, so that they carry them away captives unto the land of the enemy, far or near ;

Yet if they shall bethink themselves in the land whither they were carried captives, and repent, and make supplication unto thee in the land of them that carried them captives, saying, We have sinned, and have done perversely, we have committed wickedness ;

Then hear thou their prayer and their supplication in heaven thy dwelling place, and maintain their cause,

For they be thy people, and thine inheritance, which thou broughtest forth out of Egypt, from the midst of the furnace of iron.

And it was so that when Solomon had made an end of praying all this prayer and supplication unto the Lord, he arose from before the altar of the Lord, from kneeling on his knees with his hands spread up to heaven.

And he stood and blessed all the congregation of Israel with a loud voice, saying :

Blessed be the Lord that hath given rest unto his people Israel, according to all that he promised; there hath not failed one word of all his good promise, which he promised by the hand of Moses his servant.

The Lord our God be with us, as he was with our fathers; let him not leave us nor forsake us:

That he may incline our hearts unto him, to walk in all his ways, and to keep his commandments, and his statutes, and his judgments, which he commanded our fathers.

And let these my words, wherewith I have made supplication before the Lord, be nigh unto the Lord our God day and night, that he maintain the cause of his servant, and the cause of his people Israel at all times, as the matter shall require:

That all the people of the earth may know that the Lord is God, and that there is none else.

Let your heart therefore be perfect with the Lord our God, to walk in his statutes and to keep his commandments, as at this day.

V. PRAYER.

ALMIGHTY and most merciful God: we thank thee for the privilege granted unto us of assembling here this morning, with our psalms of praise, our thanksgiving of prayer, our words of tribute. In thy sight the centuries are but as days. The nations of this earth rise and fall, but thou art the same. May the lessons of this hour impress us with a new and deeper sense of life. We thank thee for the noble ancestry which now receives our honor. Those of old braved the ocean, conquered the wilderness, and set the free church and state in the waste land of a New World. They came impelled by the truths of Christianity to do the work for which a grateful world pays them homage. They were in the line of martyrs and reformers. These walls they reared. Here the fire of loyalty to God was fanned, here they pledged themselves to unyielding fidelity, here the vows of Christian service were made. Again we seem to see the brave, earnest faces, and hear the strong, triumphant voices that were of the first worship offered in this venerable house. We thank thee that by the power of spiritual sympathy we can ally ourselves at this hour with those of old whose lives, prayers, and labors have wrought for us such boons and privileges. We remember at this time all for whom we should pray: the weary, the sick, the tempted, — asking that the precious aid which the spirit of religion affords may be with such. We remember the homes represented here, and ask that the children in them, whose voices are as sweet music, and their faces as sunshine, may be blest in a ripening manhood and womanhood ; that the gray-haired sires may enjoy the happy retrospect of peaceful, honored old age ; that those bearing the burdens of public and private life may be strong and devoted. Make to appear now, in our thoughts, all of the past which may assist our worship and exercises at this time. Memory is busy, the heart stirs with emotion, vanished forms and hushed accents return ; turn all these impressions and feelings and recollections to our good. May the gentle presence of him so recently the shepherd of this flock seem to be with us, a benediction and an inspiration. Make us loyal to this beloved land, and quicken in us all true sentiments of love and reverence for the great institutions that ennoble our Republic. Above all, may we maintain a profound allegiance to the Christian truths to which sire and son are alike indebted for guidance here and hope hereafter. So assist us that our sins may be abandoned and our discipleship to Christ made stronger. We ask thy blessing on this service, on this beloved people, on the cause of our fathers, on the hopes of thy children everywhere, — as disciples of Jesus Christ. Amen.

VI. ORGAN RESPONSE.

VII. HYMN. (*W. P. Lunt.*)
Sung to the tune of "*Ward*"

WHEN, driven by oppression's rod,
   Our fathers fled beyond the sea,
Their care was first to worship God,
   And next to leave their children free.

Above the forest's gloomy shade
   The altar and the school appeared:
On that, the gifts of faith were laid;
   In this, their precious hopes were reared.

The altar and the school still stand,
   The sacred pillars of our trust;
And freedom's sons shall fill the land
   When we are sleeping in the dust.

Before thine altar, Lord, we bend,
   With grateful song and fervent prayer;
For thou, who wast our fathers' friend,
   Wilt make our offspring still thy care.

VIII. DISCOURSE.

IX. PRAYER.

X. HYMN. (*Pierpont.*)
Sung to the tune of "*America.*"

GONE are those great and good
Who here in peril stood,
   And raised their hymn.
Peace to the reverend dead!
The light that on their head
The passing years have shed
   Shall ne'er grow dim.

Ye temples, that to God
Rise where our fathers trod,
    Guard well your trust, —
The faith that dared the sea,
The truth that made them free,
Their cherished purity,
    Their garnered dust.

Thou high and holy One,
Whose care for sire and son
    All nature fills, —
While day shall break and close,
While night her crescent shows,
Oh let thy light repose
    On these our hills.

XI. BENEDICTION.

CHURCH IN HINGHAM, ENGLAND.

THE following sketch is taken from "An Essay towards a Topographical History of the County of Norfolk, by Francis Blomefield, Rector of Fersfield in Norfolk. London, 1805."

HINGHAM.

HINGHAM was the head town of the deanery, and at first contained 43 parishes. The deanery was taxed at 30*s* and it was in the Bishop's collation.

. . . .

The CHURCH is a good pile, the tower being very tall and large; the whole was rebuilt by *Remigius de Hethersete*, rector here, in the time of King *Edward* III. with the assistance of *John le Marshal*, his patron, who contributed much to the perfecting of the work; it is dedicated to St. *Andrew* the Apostle, and had several chapels in it, of which the most remarkable were at the ends of each isle, that on the north side being dedicated to the *Holy Trinity*, and that on the south side to the *Holy Virgin;* the others were dedicated to St. *Nicholas*, the *Nativity of the Virgin*, and to her *Assumption*, there was also a St. *Mary's* chapel by the *rood* altar, and another of St. *Mary of Pity*, and there were no less than seven gilds held in the church, *viz.* of St. *James*, *Corpus Christi*, St. *Andrew*, *Holy-Cross*, *All-Saints*, St. *John* Baptist, and St. *Mary*, and each having a stipendiary chaplain, serving at their altars in the church, constituted a choir; for in 1484, *Robert Morley*, Esq. of this town was buried in the church, and gave seven surplices to the quire of *Hingham;* and without doubt this church must make a fine appearance in those times, it being adorned with the following images, all which had lights, either lamps, wax tapers, or candles, constantly burning before them in time of divine service, and being dispersed all over the church, chancel, and chapels, must make it in the night season a fine sight; the *principal image* of St. *Andrew* stood (as the *principal image* or *Patron* saint of every church did) in the chancel, on the north side of the altar, and those of St. *Peter*, St. *Michael*, St. *Mary*, *Corpus Christi*, St. *Margaret*, St. *Christin*, St. *Edith* or *Sythe*, St. *Mary of Pity*, St. *Thomas*, the *Nativity* and *Assumption* of the *Holy Virgin*, St. *Wulstan*, St. *Appolonia*, St. *Christopher*, St. *Erasmus*, St. *Julian*, St. *Anthony*, St. *John* Baptist, St. *Nicholas*, the *Holy Trinity*, St. *Edmund*, St. *Laurence*, St. *Catherine*, St. *John* the Evangelist, St. *Valentine*, St. *Ethelred*, and the *Holy Rood* or *Cross*, which stood on the *rood-loft*, between the church and the chancel.

When *Norwich* Domesday was wrote, the patronage was late Sir *John Marshal's* but then the Lord *Morley's;* the rector had a noble house, and 20 acres of ground, the living being then valued at 50 marks; it stands in the King's Books at 24*l.* 18*s.* 4*d.* and pays 2*l.* 9*s.* 10*d.* yearly tenths, and first fruits every vacancy, it being undischarged; the synodals are 2*s.* 8*d.* and Peter-pence 1*s.* 2*d. ob.* The town paid 7*l.* each tenth.

[Then follows a list of Rectors, beginning with Master *Richard de Felmingham* in 1272; and among them appears the following : —]

1605, 7 *Jan. Robert Peck*, A.M.

ROBERT PECK.

REV. ROBERT PECK was ordained Teacher of the church Nov. 28, 1638. In the "Peck Genealogy," by Ira G. Peck, we find the following account of him: —

Rev. Robert Peck was born at Beccles, Suffolk County, England, in 1580. He was graduated at Magdalen College, Cambridge; the degree of A.B. was conferred upon him in 1599, and that of A.M. in 1603. He was set apart to the ministry, and inducted over the church at Hingham, Norfolk County, England, Jan. 8, 1605, where he remained until 1638, when he fled from the persecutions of the Church to this country.

He was a talented and influential clergyman, a zealous preacher, and a non-conformist to the superstitions, ceremonies, and corruptions of the church, for which he was persecuted and driven from the country. Brook, in his Lives of the Puritans, gives many facts of interest in relation to him. In particular, giving some of the offences for which he and his followers were persecuted, he says: "For having catechised his family, and sung a psalm in his own house on a Lord's day evening, when some of his neighbors attended, his lordship (Bishop Harsnet) enjoined all who were present to do penance, requiring them to say, 'I confess my errors,' etc."

Those who refused were immediately excommunicated and required to pay heavy costs. This, Mr. Brook says, appears from the bishop's manuscripts under his own hands. He says, "He was driven from his flock, deprived of his benefice, and forced to seek his bread in a foreign land."

He arrived here in 1638. In relation to his arrival the town clerk of Hingham here says: "Mr. Robert Peck, preacher of the gospel in the town of Hingham, in the County of Norfolk, old England, with his wife and two children and two servants, came over the sea and settled in the town of Hingham, and he was a Teacher of the Church." Mr. Hobart, of Hingham, says in his diary, that he was ordained here Teacher of the church, Nov. 28, 1638. His name frequently appears upon the records of the town. He had lands granted him. His family consisted of nine children. He remained here until the long Parliament, or until the persecutions in England ceased, when he returned and resumed his rectorship at Hingham. Mr. Hobart says he returned Oct. 27, 1641.

He died at Hingham, England, and was buried in his churchyard there.

Cotton Mather, in his " Magnalia Christi Americana," has the following : —

Mr. Robert Peck. — This light, having been by the persecuting prelates ' put under a bushel,' was, by the good providence of Heaven, fetched away into New England, about the year 1638, where the good people of our Hingham did ' rejoice in the light for a season.' But within two or three years, the invitation of his friends at Hingham in England persuaded him to a return unto them ; where being, though a great person for *stature*, yet a greater for *spirit*, he was greatly serviceable for the good of the church.

Blomefield, in his " Essay " already referred to, speaks of Robert Peck among the rectors of the church in Hingham, England. A more particular and candid account would be desirable, but we must remember the spirit which moved the writer to his work, — Blomefield being a churchman and Peck a non-conformist.

He says : —

1605, 7 *Jan. Robert Peck*, A.M. Tho. Moor, by grant of *Francis Lovell*, Knt. he was " a man of a very violent schismatical spirit, he pulled down the rails, and levelled the altar and the whole chancel a foot below the church, as it remains to this day, but being prosecuted for it by Bishop *Wren*, he fled the kingdom, and went over into *New-England*, with many of his parishioners, who sold their estates for half their value, and conveyed all their effects to that new plantation, erected a town and colonie, by the name of Hingham, where many of their posterity are still remaining, he promised never to desert them, but hearing that Bishops were deposed, he left them all to shift for themselves, and came back to *Hingham* in the year 1646, after 10 years voluntary banishment, he resumed his rectory, and died in the year 1656." His funeral sermon was preached by *Nathaniel Jocelinc*, A.M. pastor of the Church of *Hardingham*, and was published by him, being dedicated to Mr. *John Sidley*, high-sheriff, *Brampton-Gurdon* and Mr. *Day*, Justices of the Peace, Mr. *Church*, Mr. *Barnham*, and Mr. *Man*, aldermen and justices in the city of *Norwich*.

1638, 25 *May*, Luke *Skippon*, A.M. was presented by Sir THOMAS WOODHOUSE, Knt. and Bart. as on *Peck's* death, he having been absent about two years; and in

1640, 11 *April*, the said *Luke* was reinstituted, the living being void by lapse, it appearing that *Peck* was alive since *Skippon's* first institution, and now two years more being past, and he not appearing, it lapsed to the Crown, as on *Peck's* death; but in

1646,[1] *Peck* came again, and held it to his death.

[1] 1641, according to Hobart's Diary.

THE COMMUNION SERVICE.

The Communion Service comprises fourteen silver cups, three plates, and two tankards. According to the inscriptions upon the cups two were

> " The Gift of M^r
> Preserved Hall
> to ye first Church of
> Christ in Hingham."

Two were

> " The Gift of Mrs Hannah Thaxter (Relict of the Honble
> Saml. Thaxter) to the first Church of Christ in Hingham,
> 1756."

Two were

> " The Gift of Mrs Elizabeth Beal (Relict of
> Mr Daniel Beal) to the first Church in Hingham
> 1769."

Six were

> " Presented to the first Church in Hingham
> by Mrs Sarah Derby
> once the confort of Dr Ezekiel Hearsey
> 1790."

Two were

> " Bequeathed by the widow Ruth Leavitt,
> to the first Church in Hingham
> 1794."